# THE STEWARDESS'S DIARY - PART EIGHT

## HOLLAND

### S.M. PRATT

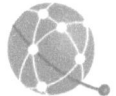

***The Stewardess's Diary - Part Eight: Holland***
Copyright © 2017 by S.M. Pratt

This is a work of fiction. Names, characters, businesses, places, events, and incidents are either the products of the author's imagination or used in a fictitious manner. Any resemblance to actual persons, living or dead, or actual events is purely coincidental.

**WARNING:** This is a work of erotic fiction and contains GRAPHIC DEPICTIONS OF SEX, WHICH MAY OFFEND SOME AUDIENCES. This book is meant for MATURE AUDIENCES AGED 18 OR OLDER (or whatever the local laws are in your area). All sexually active characters in this work are 18 years of age or older.

Last updated January 25th, 2020
Editing by Samantha Marie

ISBN: 978-1-988639-01-7 (e-book)

ISBN: 978-1-988639-27-7 (paperback)

# PROLOGUE

I'M CHARLIE, a veteran pilot for a major international airline that shall remain nameless for reasons you'll soon come to understand.

A year ago, while waiting for my flight to London in the airline's lounge at one of America's largest hubs, I discovered a special and highly personal journal among my belongings. How it happened, I'll never know, but the beautiful brown leather notebook nonetheless appeared in my briefcase at some point between the time I left my New York penthouse apartment and arrived at the airport lounge.

Perhaps it was a mix-up at security, or some devious stewardess with sly hand skills, but I've since become obsessed with the person who wrote that diary, her stories, and—to be blunt—her unconventional sex life.

My best friend—let's call him Bob—is one of my regular co-pilots. Bob advised me to forget about the journal and ignore my hunch to track down its rightful owner. After my initial reading of her hand-written accounts, the part of me who's loyal to the airline and wants the best for our passengers certainly needed to find that stewardess and expel her from our company—or whatever airline she's with. This woman is surely a threat to any crew with her irreverent disregard for our uniforms, her sexual behavior with passengers and airline employees, and the way she ignores regulations. She should clearly be punished for her conduct...

But after reading and re-reading each one of her journal entries, another, more animal part of me has grown fond of her complete lack of boundaries, her willingness to experiment, and her ravenous sexual appetite.

I've had my fair share of illicit affairs with female flight attendants and co-pilots, but none of them were interesting enough to be granted a second fuck by yours truly, let alone be courted or considered for a long-term relationship. But the woman who's filled so many pages with delicate calligraphy and salacious words deserves my full attention. She's certainly maintained it well past the time I closed the cover of her journal—again and again.

Imagining how her naiveté was gradually—and most willingly—robbed from her was simply... enthralling. She's been haunting my wet dreams.

Now, every time I see an unknown stewardess, I wonder if *she*'s the one.

After many conversations with Bob over the past months during our overseas flights, I've come to share some of her journal entries with him. He agrees that I need to locate her. If not for the airline's sake or to satisfy my personal curiosity, then for the mere reason that I could stop obsessing about her and resume paying attention to my actual job: piloting giant aircrafts and safely getting passengers from point A to point B.

The following short stories record my obsession toward her. There are ten in total. Each installment contains my mystery stewardess's original journal entries for a specific location, followed by my own experiences in trying to track her down. You'll discover what (and whom) I did in an effort to identify and locate my stewardess based on the clues she's left in her diary. You can read the episodes in any order, but they'll probably make more sense if you start from the beginning and follow along as I attempt to find her.

And, just to be clear, these stories should *not* land in the hands of any prude or underage person. Some are just romantic, sensual, or highly erotic, while others are immoral, perverse, and possibly even illegal in some parts of the world.

Ah, the things I'll do to this mystery stewardess when I finally encounter her in the flesh!

I'm hard just thinking about it...

Yours truly,

*Capt. Charlie*
Undisclosed Airline

# PART ONE

## THE STEWARDESS'S ENTRIES

11:30 A.M.

ALEX FLIPPED a coin in the air. "Heads. You drive, but I get first dibs on men."

"As you wish." I took the key the car rental agent had been patiently holding, waiting for either of us to grab. "Thanks," I told him. "We'll bring it back in one piece in a couple of days."

He smiled and nodded, then we made our way to the compact we'd rented to travel to the southern part of the Netherlands.

Alex walked in front of me wearing her knee-length skirt and curve-hugging T-shirt. The lack of straps underneath the thin fabric of her top made it clear that a bra was an optional item for her, at least today. I'm sure the car rental guy hadn't minded at all. I'd noticed his wandering eyes here and there while we discussed the contract. Let's just say that my friend's gorgeous red hair—as bold and eye-catching as it was—hadn't been the focus of his attention.

Alex and I had both traded our uniforms for comfortable summer wear a few minutes earlier. I had opted for a spaghetti-strapped dress. And based on the bright sunlight that shone above us upon leaving the Amsterdam airport, we'd chosen wisely.

*In a few hours, we'll be in Maastricht.*

I was looking forward to getting out of the capital for once, past the flat lands of the north. Alex, the one flight attendant I knew who truly enjoyed camping and other outdoor activities—and the most open-minded as well—was surely the right person to accompany me on this short adventure.

Once out of the capital and on the A2 highway, Alex folded the map the rental agency had given us then stowed it in the glove compartment.

"This is so empty and orderly compared to my car," she said after clicking the compartment shut.

"You have a car?" I asked, surprised.

"Well, technically yes... But I wouldn't dare drive it anywhere far... It needs serious repairs."

I turned to look at her briefly. "Maybe you can find yourself a mechanic with benefits," I said.

She laughed. "Yeah. I should really consider that. You have one?"

"A mechanic or a car?"

"Either..."

"No. I sold mine a while back. I wasn't spending enough time in town to make it worth my insurance premiums and parking costs."

"Yeah, but you get to see the whole world instead."

Yes, I was grateful for the flat and beautiful scenery that surrounded us right now. Thousands of miles away from home. "You're totally right. We're damn lucky... Here, right now... Would you ever considering quitting this job?" I asked Alex.

"What for? It's THE perfect job! How else could you see so much of the world AND get paid for it?"

*She isn't wrong.*

"What if you were given a unique opportunity? What if you didn't have to do much and could still make a ton of money?"

"Like marrying a billionaire? That could be interesting for a while, but I'd get bored. I mean... One dick... for the rest of my life?"

"Yeah, that could get a bit boring. But what if this opportunity came with built-in variety?"

"Like getting my own harem of billionaires?"

A giggle left my lips. "Something like that..."

"Then I'd jump on the chance to do it. Any of my wealthy sex slaves could pay for my travels around the world if I had an urge to go somewhere. But let's face it: it ain't gonna happen. Worse odds than winning the lottery. No point in dreaming about it."

*Yeah. A once in a lifetime opportunity. Should I take Nicholas's offer and settle in Paris?*

But before I could think about it some more, Alex resumed her chit-chat. "So, what's up with you these days? We didn't get much of a chance to catch up on the plane."

*Should I tell her?*

While I trusted her with my life during work, I wasn't sure I was ready to share that secret with her. After all, Nicholas had warned me the opportunity had to remain private, and Alex did enjoy gossiping...

*Better not.*

I cleared my throat. "You know... The usual—"

"Did I tell you about my last guy in Boston? All talk and no cigar. I mean, he was good with his hands and his tongue, but his dick was like this," she said.

I took my eyes off of the road for a second to look at her. She was moving her pinky up in the air.

"Oh no," I said before exploding in laughter with her. "Sorry about that."

"Well, there's only so much one can do with imagination... But I do travel with toys for these rare occurrences."

"You're braver than me. I keep mine at home, safe in my top drawer. Aren't you afraid of getting stopped and searched at customs?" I glanced at her briefly. She was shaking her head.

"Could be a great ice breaker for the customs guy if he's cute. If not, then no harm done. It would probably give whoever finds it some mental material for his next solo session... God! I'm really hoping for a well-hung Dutchman this weekend. I need to make up for it... And you, did you follow my advice?"

"Guess I never thanked you for that... Let's just say that I'm on the accelerated program now," I said.

"Much better, no?"

I nodded. "Hell yeah. I had no idea my life

could become that entertaining by making one tiny mindset shift."

"You're overthinking it. Glad to have helped. Buy me lunch and we'll call it even."

"Sure. And let's hope we find ourselves some handsome studs!"

"No doubt we will," she said before cranking up the volume on the radio.

4:30 P.M.

WHEN WE REACHED the center of Maastricht, Alex rolled down her window. A mild skunky smell wafted in the car as the heavier traffic forced us to slow to a crawl near a coffee shop.

"Hmmm," Alex said, but left it at that.

*I've never seen her smoke... Come to think of it, we've never even talked about weed. Ever.*

The traffic got moving again and she sighed. "How I'd love some of that," she finally said, breaking the silence.

"I was thinking the same." I smiled and briefly turned to look at her. Her eyes were round, one eyebrow higher than the other. I returned my eyes to the road in front of me.

"You?" she exclaimed.

"Why not?"

"First you learn to embrace my type of relationships with men... And now... My type of occasional entertainment as well? I'm impressed with my little *protégée*. I thought the possibility of random testing would have you scared shitless."

"At first I was... Then I found a way to circumvent the results."

"Who told you?"

"Good ole Google pointed me to a helpful forum. The reviews for these cleansing kits had me adding them to my cart in no time. Have yet to be tested, though. Unsure if they'll really work, or if it's all a big marketing scam and I'll lose my job."

"For the record, they do work. At least the one I used during my last test... I came out clean."

"That's a relief." *Then again, I do have another job opportunity waiting for me if I were to fail one of those tests...*

"So, what do you say?" she asked, tapping me on the arm and bringing me back to the present moment.

"When in Rome... Let's enjoy some of the local delicacy!"

Alex clapped and let out a few high-pitch screams of joy.

Tired from the red-eye leg I'd worked hours ago, but wanting to have a good time, I wondered what was more important. "Should we do that before finding a hotel room?" I asked Alex.

"Way to go, girl! I'd say your priorities are right. There'll be lots of time to find a hotel and bike rental shop after our first stop."

I PARKED the car and we backtracked on foot to the coffee shop we'd seen a few minutes earlier. For those who'd lost their sense of smell, the telltale sticker was displayed in the window.

I followed Alex in. The place wasn't as packed as I'd assumed it would be.

*But then again, people do work on weekdays, and we're far away from tourist-packed Amsterdam.*

"Hi. Can I get a couple of grams of whatever is popular?" Alex asked the tall blond man behind the counter.

"Do you have your resident *cart*?" he asked, rolling his R and confusing me by using the word *cart*.

But it seemed Alex was better with his accent. "A card? I thought weed cards were no longer needed?"

He shook his head. "With *de* new regulations, we can't sell to tourists. Only residents."

Upon overhearing the disappointing news, I stopped looking at the accessories and got closer to Alex at the counter. "But I read online that most places don't ask for it," I said. "Can't we just order a little weed? No questions asked?"

"Well, *dat*'s true in Amsterdam and most of Holland. But here in Maastricht..." He shook his head again. "*Dey* have cracked down. Because of Belgium and Germany being so close, local law makers have different views on drug tourism. I cannot do it. Sorry."

I took a step toward the exit, but Alex didn't follow me. I turned around and saw her lean forward on the counter. She showed the cute man her biggest smile. "But isn't there a way you can make an exception for two lovely, out-of-town flight attendants?"

She stepped aside, pulled me by the elbow, then brought me closer to her. "We're only going to be here in your beautiful country for a few days..."

He looked behind Alex to the other customers.

A couple got up and exited the store, leaving just two young men who couldn't be older than twenty.

"I could get in trouble..." he said.

"Come on, there's hardly anyone in your shop right now. We're not with the government. We're not going to report you." Alex looked around at the remaining customers, then lowered her voice. "These two potheads definitely don't look like they work... for anyone... let alone your government."

He let out a long sigh, looked at me, then looked at Alex again.

*Maybe?* I walked back to the counter. *Strength in numbers and all of that.*

But instead of using her words to push him over the edge, Alex pulled down on the stretchy fabric of her T-shirt and leaned onto the counter.

"Can I convince you to bend the rules, just this once?" she asked as she ran a couple of fingers down her exposed cleavage.

"Are you girls... a couple?" he asked, totally out of the blue.

"No," Alex said, shaking her head. "I mean, I like her, but not *that* much. We're just two single women..." Her hand went up to his face and, with one finger, she traced the outline of his bearded jaw. "Looking for a good time," she added.

He cleared his throat then licked his lower lip. "Well... Maybe," he said. "It depends on how convincing you are." He looked at me and his eyebrows went up, as if asking me to join my friend.

I undid the first two buttons of my sundress.

He leaned over the counter and lowered his voice. "Maybe I will help you, but I will need to see more than *dat*," he said, pointing at our (still mostly covered) breasts.

The doorbell chimed again. The two young men who'd been sitting at the table behind us had left.

"Show me your tits, and I'll see what I can do," he said, this time a little louder since we were the only ones left in the shop.

I looked at Alex. She raised her shoulders. I unbuttoned the rest of my dress's delicate buttons. As if we'd practiced our timing, she pulled up her T-shirt exactly when I pulled my breasts out of my dress's built-in support. He took a good look, his tongue almost dangling out of his open mouth. Just as his hands reached toward us, the doorbell chimed again, and I covered up. Alex had done the same. I began doing up my buttons as fast as I could.

"Stefan," a deep voice said behind us. Then words were spoken in what I assumed was Dutch.

"Bram, come meet *dese* two," he said to the man that had just walked in before returning his attention to us. "He's my *broder* Bram."

My dress fully done up, I turned around. The men were obviously identical twins. Both had the same blond hair, the same beard, the same beautiful blue eyes. The only difference I could see was that the guy behind the counter wore a blue shirt, and the other one, a red shirt.

The man behind the counter—the one who'd just seen our tits—extended his hand. "My name is Stefan," he said.

We shook hands, then Alex turned around and started chatting with the newly arrived brother.

I paid for our two grams and some rolling paper while no other customers were in the store. Stash in hand, I walked over to the nearest table and was opening my baggie when Stefan called out to me. "I'm sorry, but you cannot smoke it here."

"But I thought..." I said, confused.

"I'd like to let you, but if someone comes in and sees tourists here, I'll be in really big trouble."

Alex joined in the conversation. "But we don't have a house here, not even a hotel room."

"Well..." Stefan looked at his brother. "Maybe *dat* can be solved. Bram and I live near here. Would you like to join us *dere?*"

"But what about the shop?" I asked.

He shrugged. "We own it. Locals can go elsewhere. *Dey* know where *de* other coffee shops are. I will close. You wait outside, and *den* we go to our place. How does *dat* sound?"

Everyone seemed to agree with Stefan's suggestion.

WE FOLLOWED the handsome men down the street; I enjoyed staring at their tight asses in their jeans as they led the way. They probably cycled—or fucked—a lot to get such firm-looking butts. Or maybe they swam?

Their wide shoulders, their narrow hips, their long legs... Everything seemed identical. And so tempting... I could only imagine their naked bodies cutting through water in beautiful butterfly strokes.

*Damn I'm horny!*

"I will grab some beers and snacks and meet you in *de* flat," Bram said to Stefan. His bothering to talk to his brother in English made me feel comfortable. *How hospitable of them both.*

A few minutes later, Stefan led Alex and me up a narrow staircase. He unlocked his door and let us into their apartment.

"Make yourselves at home." He pointed to the bean bags that littered the living room, then walked over to his stereo system and cranked up some reggae before plugging in a lava lamp. "Please sit," he said. "I'll be right back."

Alex and I looked at each other. I raised my shoulders.

It had been a while since I'd last seen a bean bag...

*But who am I to define what qualifies as grown-up furniture? Maybe the lovely twins are younger than I think? Maybe real living room furniture is expensive in Holland?*

"Why the heck not?" I said as I threw myself on the nearest makeshift seat.

Alex moseyed around the room, looking at various paper posters that had been taped to the walls. In the process, she picked up, inspected, then put down the odd trinkets that rested on the sparse furniture. Bob Marley and cannabis leaves were definitely a recurring theme in their decor.

"Stop snooping around and sit," I said.

She raised her shoulders, then slouched on the bean bag directly opposite me, across from the tiny coffee table in the middle. On second glance, it was more of a nightstand. It had a drawer on one side, and its height would have been perfect next to a bed. I resisted the urge to pull the drawer open.

Stefan came back with a bong and sat on the bean bag in front of that drawer, between Alex and me, just as his brother entered the apartment. Bram came toward us and handed us a cold can of Heineken each, then he was off to another room, possibly to store the remaining beers in a fridge somewhere.

I cracked mine open, then clanked it against Alex's, then Stefan's.

"Cheers!" we all said.

The liquid cooled my parched throat, but I did my best not to finish it all in a few sips.

A moment later, Bram joined us in the living room and sat on one of the unoccupied bean bags across from his brother. He dropped a bowl of black licorice on the nightstand, along with a small bag of chips, unopened.

*Sweet and salty snacks! I'm so hungry.*

Bram picked up a couple of licorice pieces then pointed to the bowl. "Have some."

I was starving, so I did. The piece I put in my

mouth was harder than I expected it to be, and its salty bitterness made me wince. But a few seconds later, I got used to the taste and began to slowly chew my way through it.

A lovely, familiar scent started to fill the room. Stefan had used his own stash to fill the bong with smoke, inhaled some, then passed the device to Alex. Soon enough, a cloud of smoke had formed above our heads.

Another round of beers was offered—and accepted, of course. A boring and long-winded conversation about the beauty of what Alex had seen to date in the Netherlands began (although her many double entendres probably went unnoticed by Bram, whose thigh Alex's hand rested on.)

I tuned her out, enjoying my increasingly potent high instead. That is until Bram opened the bag of chips; the crackling sound got my stomach's attention. "Yes, we are very lucky here in Holland," he said.

He ate a couple of chips then passed the bag to Alex. "Why did you come here instead of Amsterdam?" he asked her.

"It was her idea," she said, her hand in the bag while nodding my way.

The two handsome men now had their dilated pupils glued on me.

I raised my shoulders. "I've already visited Amsterdam a few times. It's beautiful and everything, but I think stepping outside of the capital is better if I want to see what the real Holland is like. Don't you agree?"

Stefan nodded while Bram inhaled from the bong.

It seemed like Alex couldn't care less about what I was saying. Her hand was now resting higher on Bram's thigh. Or was it Stefan's? I'd lost track of which twin had the red shirt on.

"Anyway, we're going to rent bikes and camping gear tomorrow morning and explore the countryside around here. I haven't ridden a bike in so long. Can't wait to feel the wind in my hair, inhale the fresh air while soaking in the beautiful scenery."

"Is there something we definitely have to see while we're here?" Alex asked. "We've only got two nights and two days before we fly out."

"You're looking at our country's finest right here," the twin who was closest to Alex said with a smirk, pointing at his brother and himself. He then turned to Alex and tapped on his own lap. "Have a closer inspection if you want."

She took him up on his offer, but instead of sitting on his lap, she landed flat next to him, then rolled off the bean bag onto the floor before exploding in laughter. A few seconds later, he reorganized the extra bean bags and they started making out like horny teenagers.

I was pretty high and happy. And now, with Alex's intentions out in the open—and two hot guys within reach—it looked like finding a hotel room for the night may not be something worth worrying about.

The available twin turned to me and smacked his lips onto mine before rolling on top of me. His lips tasted of salty licorice and his cologne smelled of sea salt. His hand grabbed my breasts and I let him feel his way under my sundress while I reached for his hard body. His firm buttocks didn't disappoint. I slid a hand up onto his lean, muscular back while my other hand squeezed itself between our bodies as I went for the solid bumps on his stomach. *Holy shit! Talk about a real, hard six-pack!*

As though he had read my mind, he pulled away from me for a second, then took off his T-shirt, exposing his hairless, sculpted torso. I think that's when my panties got flash flooded—or at least, that's when I noticed how drenched they were.

"I'm starving," I heard the other twin say.

And just like that, our make-out session was put on hold. My twin got up and walked over to a stack of papers on the corner of a table in the corner.

"Pizza?" he asked.

We all nodded. The high had me—and probably all of us—starving now. And not just for food. Alex licked her lips, but I'm pretty sure pizza wasn't what was on her mind either.

We smoked some more—this time from my recently purchased stash—while waiting for the pizza to arrive.

When it did, I was surprised to find it topped with lamb, but it tasted awesome.

Somehow the conversation had returned to flower fields and cycling, but after what felt like an hour of relentless talking, Alex interrupted her twin by jumping on him and kissing him half-way through his current point.

"Okay. Enough said," he said as soon as he could catch a breath.

He got up, pulled Alex by the hand, and

escorted her out of the living room, leaving me alone with my twin, who didn't wait a second to kiss me.

His lips were even more succulent with the added saltiness of the pizza on them.

BEANS SHIFTED in my twin's chair, then his hand landed on my waist before it began inching its way toward my breasts.

"My brother's going to fuck your friend real nice."

I looked at him: he was smiling, and lust sparkled in his beautiful blue eyes.

"And what are *you* going to do to me?"

His hands groped my breasts, he squeezed and massaged them through the fabric like they were Play-Doh. He locked eyes again and brought his hands to my face before replying. "It depends... What do you want?"

"Get fucked real nice...?" I asked, partly mocking him, but then again not. My sex talk in Dutch was non-existent and I wanted to fuck him so desperately.

Without a word more, he landed on my limp body. I could feel his readiness through his jeans as his lips swallowed mine, and his hands went right for my breasts again.

"Careful with the buttons!" I said, trying to squeeze my hands underneath his to undo the delicate pearl-like pieces before his strong hands would rip them off.

He got up and off from me for a second to take off his belt. I stared at his hairless chest, strong pecks, and six-pack abs... No, it was an eight-pack!

While I could have easily stared at the beautiful man in front of me for ages, I chose to take off my dress and get this party going. I flung it somewhere on the floor, but I didn't have time to remove my panties before his warm, hard body landed back on top of me.

I let my fingers run down his muscular back and my pussy warmed up even more. I swear my libido had morphed into a ticking bomb. I slid a hand between our bodies, eager to caress his abs, then went further south until I reached the waist of his jeans. His erect cock pushed itself up against the thick fabric. *Poor thing...* I managed to undo his button and zipper with a little pull of his hips, then I dove in to grab the body part that needed rescuing.

"Commando!" I said.

He moaned something, then his hands tried to pull my panties down. I lifted my ass for a second to clear the way.

Then, our fingers competed—or collaborated—in mixed confusion to get his jeans off in record time. He rolled off of me for a second before his hand fumbled through the drawer of the nightstand-turned-coffee-table.

A few seconds later, he proudly waved what he'd been looking for: a condom.

*That's what they keep in there?*

Without losing a second, and before I could offer to roll it onto him, he covered his glorious appendage and leaned back against my body.

He kissed me, his twirling tongue only serving to poke at my already blazing embers of desire. I wrapped my hand around his cock and aimed it at my swollen pussy. He appeared to have gotten my message loud and clear as his mouth pulled away, then his upper body did the same. He parted my legs some more and a crooked smile appeared on his face as he stared at my pussy.

"Fuck me already!" I ordered.

And he obeyed, tenderly at first. He barely inserted the tip, then he slowly pushed the rest of his huge cock into my welcoming pussy. Every delicious inch of his impressive girth smoothly slid into me, parting my insides. His cock was the oasis my aching pussy had been longing for all day. I let a moan escape my lips, and he grunted in reply before picking up the tempo. My excitement grew to the soundtrack of our bodies meshing over the moving beans below us.

I let my hands explore his back before settling on his firm ass so I could push him deeper into me. Every now and then he grunted a few Dutch words I didn't understand. I couldn't care less about what he was saying. He could have been calling me names for all that it mattered; it wouldn't have changed how fast he was bringing me to heaven's gates.

I pulled back a bit, trying to slow down the inevitable and stretch the blissful moment we were sharing. I reached for his face, and my fingers landed on the soft beard that covered his square jaw. Our gazes met and his blue eyes had me hypnotized. While he kept pounding me, his warm and hard muscles forcing themselves against my softer body, I had to kiss his lips, my tongue had to explore his mouth. It was as though kissing him allowed me to drink up some of his youth, some of his strength. The softness of his beard against my face was delightful. It wasn't scruffy, it was just fuzzy and soft... almost silkily so.

When I started quivering, I realized I had dug my nails in his back, so I let go of him and brought my hand to my clit instead. I feverishly toyed with my pleasure center as my body convulsed out of control, taking my mind to nirvana while my soul and body rejoiced in ecstasy. Now hot, sweaty, and totally relaxed from having just come, my body turned to putty in his large hands.

But he had yet to come.

He was going on and on, strong like an insatiable Energizer bunny, ramming into me so hard I though the seams of the bag would break and beans would start pouring out.

"Turn around," he said as he got off from me.

I complied and ended up with my stomach and

breasts resting on the bean bag and my hands and knees on the floor.

He moved the nightstand away then knelt behind me. His cock found its way back into my pussy, and he held on to my hips as he pounded me. I didn't know if it was the flapping noises or his incomprehensible Dutch mumbling, but he once again had me at the cusp of exploding.

"Don't stop! I'm about to come..." I said.

He thrust deeper into me for a few more seconds, then I was done for.

I let out a loud but partly muffled cry, my face in the bean bag as my limbs went limp. He was still pounding me... *Seriously? Is this man a machine?* I heard water running somewhere in the distance.

"Want some water?" he asked, pulling out of me unexpectedly.

"Sure," I said, suddenly realizing how dry my mouth was. And honestly, at that point, my pussy also deserved a short intermission.

I flipped myself around and stared at the ceiling fan that hung motionless above me while waiting for my well-hung Dutch lover to return. My high was still straddling the atmosphere even though the cloud of smoke had long dissipated.

I thought of my friend for a second, and could

only imagine that these twins were identical in all ways.

*I'm happy she's getting fucked by a big one this time, just like she wanted.*

My fingers played with my clit as I waited for him to return. While my pussy was a little sore, my nub had proven to be more resilient... It wasn't like my excitement was going to dissipate if I didn't play with myself, but what else was I going to do?

He came back a few minutes later, a tall glass of water in hand. Seemed he'd disposed of the condom while in the kitchen. *Did he come without me noticing?* I quenched my thirst and handed the glass back to the beautiful man in front of me.

A few seconds later, we were back to where we'd been minutes ago. His glorious erect cock once again dressed for action, and me back on all fours, resting on the bean bag.

This time though, after poking his cock in me, he slid his hands under my breasts and unfolded my upper body so it rested against his warm, chiseled chest. I bent forward a bit to feel him more deeply as he rammed into me, his chest pressed against my back, his fingers pinching my nipples as his palms squished my breasts hard with every thrust. Not so hard that it was painful, but definitely harder than anyone had ever done it before.

He breathed hard behind me, an animalistic grunt that kept getting louder and coarser. I reached back and grabbed his ass with one hand while my other went between my legs in search of his balls. I cupped them, letting my arm move to his rhythm, then I pushed upward and squeezed them slightly as I pressed on that sensitive spot just behind them.

And it seemed to work. He tensed up and screamed something just as he came, filling me with his warmth, which had thankfully been held in the condom he withdrew a second later.

He slapped me on the ass and I let my body fall on the bean bag in front of me before turning around to look at him. He opened the coffee table drawer and took out a small box of tissues, which he offered to me.

"Thanks," I said after stealing a kiss from him.

I wiped myself then leaned back on the bean bag, totally spent.

He got up and walked away to dispose of the condom and my used tissues, then came back to fondle my breasts some more. This time, a little more gently. I couldn't help but run my fingers up and down his chiseled abs, then his strong pecks. That's when I noticed a brown spot near his left nipple: a small birthmark I hadn't seen before.

The oddly-timed water break...

The different, slightly more violent approach...

But exhausted and fulfilled, I couldn't care less if these guys shared everything.

I WOKE up on my bean bag, still naked but with a cotton sheet on my body. The birth-marked twin was lying on his back next to me, his perfectly sculpted chest slowly rising and sinking to the rhythm of his breath.

After a quick shower and coffee, we left Bram and Stefan's apartment, eager to get breakfast, rent our bicycles, and go explore the countryside. And based on the shade of pink on Alex's cheeks, I assumed she'd enjoyed an early morning session with her twin.

I felt a little bad for no longer knowing which one was which, but I knew it didn't really matter as we likely weren't going to see them again.

*Best to avoid the awkward conversation and part ways on a good note.*

Following the twins' recommendations, we rented bikes and camping gear from a nearby store, then off we went, following the route the shop attendant had recommended to us.

Even though this part was hillier than the north, the ride itself wasn't difficult. But my ass hadn't ridden a bike in a while, so I was grateful for my large padded seat.

I enjoyed the fresh breeze as we cycled out of the city. We passed through several small towns, and Alex insisted we visit one of the windmills. I'd never been one for touring buildings, so I let her enjoy her visit while I found a nearby corner store and got some more water and a bottle of wine for tonight.

I was glad once we got back on the road again.

All day, fellow cyclists passed us by. Some were touring, others zooming by on their racing bikes.

We stopped at a cafe in a small village in early afternoon, ordered a sandwich and a cold beer, then returned to our saddles with an extra sandwich each to eat that night.

WHEN THE AFTERNOON neared its end, we decided to look for a spot where we could set up our tent and relax.

Having previously ignored the last few campground signs—and the map telling us we still had a long way to go before reaching the next one —we decided we'd just pitch our tent somewhere along the road. In a way, I liked the idea. We'd be away from larger groups and potentially loud, drunken behavior. But I knew I would miss the facilities once I had to squat in the bushes to pee.

A few minutes later, we saw the perfect spot: a beautiful patch of grass along the driveway to a farm, with a nearby group of large trees that would be perfect for our bodily needs.

We made our way along the thick bush hedges and up the driveway to the two-story white, half-timbered farmhouse, passing a smaller building that I assumed was used to store various farming equipment. We knocked and waited for someone to answer.

A man in his late forties came to the door, a tired and surprised look on his angular, sun-kissed face. He looked like he'd worked hard all his life. I let Alex take care of the conversation.

"Hello," Alex said.

"*Hallo*," he replied.

"Sorry to bother you. Do you speak English?" she asked.

He frowned. "Yes."

"My friend and I were wondering if we could set up our tent on your land, just for tonight," she said, her hand indicating our overloaded bicycles standing on their footrests in the man's driveway.

The man looked at the bikes, then Alex, then me.

I smiled but kept quiet.

He finally spoke up. "Well... This is not a request I hear every day. Is it just the two of you?"

Alex and I nodded.

"Fine, as long as you clean up before you go."

"We will, of course. Thank you, sir!"

WE RETURNED to the spot that would be our campground for the night and began unloading our bikes.

I was working on setting up the tent when Alex called out to me.

"We forgot to refill our water," she said.

"Do you want me to cycle back to the nearest village?" I suggested, mentally trying to remember how long ago it was. *Not that far? But that last big hill...*

"Nah..." She paused for a second and we both looked toward the house. The farmer was standing outside, near his door, drinking from a cup and looking at us. "Let me ask Mr. Hot Farmer," she said, winking at me.

"Ah! So, you're into older men now?" I said, teasing her.

"He's not *that* old. And I bet his body looks fantastic." Her brows went up and her mouth rose into a slanted grin. "With his manual labor and all... I can only imagine what his back and strong arms must feel like..."

She pulled the near-empty bottles from both our bikes and headed back up the driveway to the house. "Be right back... or not," she yelled out to me.

I continued my tasks and had the tent set up, pads unrolled and sleeping bags ready to go before she got back. The tent now erect in front of me wasn't what I would describe as spacious, but we'd opted for the lightest and smallest gear since we didn't want to overload our bikes or wear huge backpacks.

*I hope tonight won't prove me wrong.*

Alex finally came back just as I was digging out the extra sandwiches we'd purchased at lunch and the bottle of wine I'd gotten this morning.

"Guess what?" she said.

I raised my shoulders.

"Our farmer invited us to join him for dinner. Well... Not really, but I told him we had our own food, so we'll eat what we brought and he'll cook something. Potluck-style I guess. Don't you dare touch that just yet!" She grabbed the sandwiches from my hand and put them back in one of our bikes' panniers. "We'll relax for a couple of hours, then he'll have a table set for all of us."

My growling stomach wanted to disagree, but I played along. "Should we go and help him then?"

"No, I offered. And you won't believe what I saw out back, behind the house..."

I had no idea what could have gotten her so excited. "An outhouse?" I guessed, although I had no reason to believe such a large, nice-looking house would NOT be fitted with running water and other modern amenities. I probably had my camper's hat on and the nearby bushes didn't have me so excited about the prospect.

"No, silly!" She shook her head at me. "A hot tub!"

"Really?"

Her eyes were now the size of nickels, and I swear drool was close to coming out of her mouth. "And now I officially call dibs." Her hand went up. "I kind of like Farmer John."

"John? Is that his name?"

"Nah. He's called something unpronounceable.

He gave me permission to call him John instead. I'm sure you can call him that, too."

"Farmer John is all yours then." My stomach growled again. I had to do something to keep myself from biting into our sandwiches before dinner. "What shall we do now? Go for a walk?" But saying it aloud made me realize my legs needed a break. I didn't feel like walking at all.

"Do you still have some of your weed?"

"I do..."

A few minutes later, after Alex had convinced me that I'd be able to manage my hunger even after smoking a joint, we were lying with our backs on the grass, still wearing our shorts and tank tops, looking at the clouds above us. We slowly enjoyed the joint I'd rolled, our scented puffs adding a thin layer of quickly disappearing cloud around us. There was hardly a breeze at ground level although the oddly shaped clouds moved rapidly in the higher atmosphere.

"So, what else did you find out about Farmer John?" I passed her the joint.

"Nothing really. But I asked if there was a missus. He said his wife passed away last year." She paused, then a big puff came out of her lips. "The poor man has been living alone since."

I couldn't believe how easy it was for her to flirt with anyone and everyone. "And he shared all of that information with you while you were fetching water?"

"Well... You know me. One question led to another. I saw a picture of a beautiful woman in his living room, so I asked."

I took the joint she held up and I smoked some more. "Personal boundaries and privacy don't mean anything to you?"

"Sometimes. But I wanted to know if Farmer John was available for a late-night interlude... I like sleeping under the stars, but not as much as I like getting fucked by a hot guy."

"The twins didn't do it for you?"

"*My* twin you mean? That was just *one* guy. Call me greedy, but I'd like to sample a bit more of the Dutch population..."

"For the record, you did *both* of them."

She sat up. "What? Are you kidding me?"

"No. Didn't you notice they'd traded places last night?"

"What?" she asked again, this time almost shrieking.

"One had a birth mark near his left nipple. The other didn't."

She stared at me. "I don't believe it..."

I didn't budge and added a nod to emphasize my point.

"Well... I'd like to sample three instead of just two," she said, trying to inhale, but the joint was no longer lit. "Where's the lighter?"

"In the tent, just by the zipper."

And time flew by as I admired nature's incredible beauty in the shape of the clouds alone. Birds sang their last repertoire as the shades of evening skies slowly took over. My hunger had seemingly fallen to the back-burner, until it came back with a vengeance.

AS PROMISED, Farmer John had set up a table for us on the large patio made out of interlocking stones behind his house.

On one side, close to a cluster of trees on a slight hill, two wooden swings hung, attached to a beam that had been nailed to the largest trunks. On the other side, near the table, a large hot tub presided on the backyard from the top of its elevated platform.

Unlike Alex, I hadn't seen any part of his house or his backyard to date, but it was not what I had expected for an average-looking house in the countryside.

"Nice hot tub!" I said, handing him the bottle of wine we'd brought.

"Thank you. A waste of money, I think, but my wife had insisted on getting it. Feel free to use it if you want. I keep it clean and ready for use, out of habit. Maybe we can all enjoy it after dinner?" he suggested, his eyes locked on Alex.

Her face lit up. "Wonderful idea. I'd love to!"

John invited us to sit down around the table while he went back into the house.

"Did you bring a swimsuit?" I asked Alex while our host was in the house.

"No, but I'm not planning on wearing anything in there. We're in Europe, don't be such a prude."

"No big deal, but I wouldn't want to distract him from you," I said with a large grin. "Just kidding. He's all yours. I'm pretty sure you'll get what you want."

"Let's hope so." Her eyes lit up when he came out of the house again, with three glasses held upside down by the stems in one hand and the cork-opener in the other. "Life is all about fun, isn't it?" Alex asked him.

"All about fun?" Farmer John repeated as he sat at our table.

I couldn't imagine any farmer seeing life as

complete fun... "There are a lot of fields around here. What do you grow?" I asked him.

"Corn, sugar beets, and potatoes."

"We saw some miniature horses nearby. Are they yours?" Alex asked.

"No, they belong to Niek, my neighbor. I don't have animals here. I used to have a dog, but he passed away around the same time my wife did. That's all probably very boring to two beautiful women like you. Why are you in this part of Holland?"

And Alex began chit-chatting about nothing and everything while I did my best to restrain my appetite and not stuff my sandwich down in two seconds. He'd made a large bowl of a potato-based dish he'd called *Stamppot*, and I helped myself to a generous serving of it.

"That's surprisingly delicious!" I complimented him before taking another bite.

"Surprising because…?" he asked.

I pointed to my mouth as I slowly finished chewing, mentally trying to figure out how to answer his question without offending him. Although delicious for real, the dish looked like what a person would throw up right after eating potatoes, hotdogs, and green leafy vegetables.

"Because most men I know do not fare well in the kitchen," I finally said.

He smiled widely, and relief washed over me. "It's very easy to make. You boil potatoes, onions, vegetables, and sausage together, then you mash it all when it's cooked."

"Ah! Well, simple and really tasty."

He poured us all more wine and the conversation moved on to another topic. Then another bottle was opened, even though all the food was long gone.

"Any chance I can use your bathroom?" I asked, my bladder about to explode.

"Yes, go ahead," he said. "On your left when you go in."

I thoroughly enjoyed the luxury of peeing indoors, then refreshed myself a bit and splashed my face with water. My hair looked messy from a day of riding my bike. I couldn't blame it on a helmet, since I hadn't worn one, but the breeze (and lying in the grass earlier) had obviously impacted my ponytail. I tied it up again, then walked back outside to find Farmer John and Alex sitting closer together. He had one hand on her arm over the table while his other, closer arm was hidden from view.

"Should we try the hot tub?" asked Alex when she saw me.

"Excellent idea," he said. "I'll take the dishes inside. Go ahead and get in."

"Do you need help?" I offered, reaching for one of the plates on the table.

He swatted my hand away. "No, no. I'll take care of it. I insist," he said.

*Decent cook and not afraid of domestic chores—Farmer John's a good man!*

Alex and I took off our sweaty tank tops and shorts. While I hesitated for a split second before taking off my sports bra and panties, Alex didn't, so I followed suit. I'd come a long way in getting rid of my inner prude, but I still had my moments of doubt. We walked up the steps and entered the clear but motionless water and took a seat in it, kitty-corner from each other in the four-person molded tub.

"I wonder how you make the jets go," Alex said before sitting up slightly and turning her attention to the controls.

"Shouldn't we wait for him to come back and turn it on?"

"Nah. I can figure it out." She pressed a few buttons, then lights came on, illuminating our naked bodies. A second later, a soft purring noise started and then got a little louder as the water started moving. Jets came out from seemingly everywhere. Two strong streams hit my lower back, quickly soothing away my soreness from the day's ride. I was impressed at how powerful the jets were considering their quietness.

Seemingly pleased that she had adjusted all the settings to her liking, Alex leaned back in her seat again, then pulled herself up a bit, taking her breasts out of the water and bringing her ass up to what I assumed was the jets' height.

"Now we're talking!" she said, her lips widening into a smile as she closed her eyes.

"I see you figured out how to turn it on," said Farmer John behind me.

I turned around. He was walking toward us, three folded towels in hand. A large grin had pushed away the tired expression from his face. He put down his goods at the top of the steps, then proceeded to match our birthday-suit dress code. He pulled his T-shirt over his head, exposing a very white but muscular torso, complete with abdominal muscles that could have been featured on the cover of Men's Health magazine, if only they'd been slightly more tanned, and his vertical line of dark hairs more trimmed. I looked away as he unzipped his pants, but his large, flaccid appendage caught my eyes a few seconds later when he stepped into the tub, then lowered himself on the seat next to Alex.

Her eyes met mine and, based on how wide her eyes were, I was certain we shared the same thought at that very moment. *If his cock's this big while limp, what will it turn into when he gets excited?*

"So, do you have a lot of parties here?" asked Alex.

Farmer John laughed before shaking his head. "No. Can't say that many people randomly invite themselves like you did today."

"Well... We only asked to sleep on your lawn, then you invited us back here."

He wrapped his arm around Alex's shoulders. "Even if I enjoy my simple and tranquil life, it's hard to see beautiful women like you and not want to know them better.

"Is this what you'd like? Getting to know me better?" Alex cooed as she reached for his angular jaw and brought his face closer to hers.

Then, the awkward feeling of being a third wheel started taking over. And being a third wheel in a hot tub wasn't necessarily the most comfortable environment... But then I heard something.

At first, I couldn't identify it, but as the melody repeated once more, I recognized it through the soft purring of the hot tub: my phone was ringing.

*Saved by the bell, of sorts.*

"I'll go and get that," I said, partly curious as to who would be calling me on this number and partly relieved to have an easy out to let them make out without me staring at them.

I got up, grabbed a towel on my way out, wrapped it around my dripping body, and then headed toward the tent.

I was grateful Farmer John's land was covered in grass and not pointy rocks that would have hurt my feet, but the day's humidity had condensed on the grass. By the time I reached my device in one of the panniers, it had gone silent. I looked at my missed calls and didn't recognize the number. I dialed it and waited.

Nothing. Just endless ringing.

I decided to give the caller a few minutes of grace, in the event he or she would try again, so I rolled myself a joint. Then, having it ready to go, I figured that I might as well smoke it under the beautiful evening sky. I unzipped the tent and pulled my mat out so I could rest on it instead of the wet grass. I lay back, put in my headset and listened to whatever Spotify wanted to play for me while I lit my ticket to the stars.

*Life's so fucking great right now. Just endless possibilities, like the number of shining specks that sparkled in the sky above.*

With each inhalation, any sign of remaining tension flew out of my body, heading toward the starry emptiness of the sky. The evening was so beautiful. So peaceful. Insects in the distance were doing their thing, singing their mating calls or whatever it was they did that created such beautiful nighttime noises.

A few minutes later, totally buzzed, I suddenly felt an urge to drink something. *Water?* No, I wanted wine. *I think there's some left on the table?*

I returned my mat to its rightful spot in my tent, knowing fair well that I would regret it later if I didn't do it now. I zipped the tent back up. Satisfied that my phone wouldn't ring again, I left it behind in one of my panniers then headed back to the patio the same way I'd come.

When I got there, Alex and Farmer John were in the midst of a passionate kiss so I let them have their privacy, kind of.

I poured myself the glass I craved, then went to sit in one of the swings a short distance away, after almost tripping on one of the exposed roots as I walked up the slight hill. The only light on me was that of the moon and stars above. On the other hand, Alex and Farmer John were illuminated by the underwater lights as well as the motion-activated light fixture above the back door.

I had my own private show, and my seat was perfectly positioned to see everything that was happening in that tub. Knowing Alex and her tendency toward exhibitionism—as I had found out in Toronto—I was certain she'd be totally fine with me watching them.

So I did.

I slowly sipped my wine while my toes pushed and pulled my body forward on the swing. I was already buzzed, so my slight movements were more than plenty for my mind.

With a splashing sound, Farmer John pulled Alex out of the water before sitting her down on the wooden deck that surrounded the tub. Her legs dangled against the back of the seat she had previously occupied. Then he knelt between her legs on the seat in front of her. He grabbed her generous breasts and buried his head in them, moaning loudly, the muffled sound easily reaching my ears. His balding head bobbed while his large hands squeezed her breasts together around his face as though he was trying to suffocate himself into Alex's fleshy goods. Then he pulled his head out, grabbed a handful of her right breast, then started licking it. He pinched her nipple, shaping it into a small raspberry, and she moaned while arching her back, her breasts coming closer toward him.

He slowly let go of her right breast and repeated his routine with the other before slowly licking his way down her flat ivory stomach. When he reached her belly button, she parted her legs farther apart and looked back at him again. He stepped back, then buried his face between her legs. He brought one of her legs to rest above his shoulder. Every now and then, I could see his tongue licking her clean-shaven pussy, then disappearing into her. My friend's moans were merging with those of the animal kingdom around us, getting louder and louder. Then, as though the poor man had to come up for air, his body unfolded and I got my first glimpse at his monster dick.

My hand flew to my mouth to repress my surprised gulp. It must have been a solid ten-inch stick, bigger than I had ever seen. Even bigger than the twins' cocks had been.

He reached into the pants he'd taken off earlier and dug a condom out from one of the pockets. A second later, his tool had been made weatherproof and ready for action. That was too much voyeurism for me to take in idly. I leaned down to place my empty glass on the grass near my feet, then parted my legs. With one arm holding my body steady on the swing, I started fingering myself.

Unsurprisingly, I was already dripping wet, so wet that Farmer John and Alex could have probably heard the slick movements of my fingers in and out of me if not for their own excited moans and groans over the super-quiet tub's purring noises. Somehow my towel untied itself, my parted legs having probably caused it to happen. I let the damp fabric fall as it may, and the evening air started to caress my newly exposed back, stomach, and breasts. My nipples hardened from the change in temperature, and a shiver crossed my entire body like an out-of-control tornado.

Farmer John brought the tip of his cock toward my friend's pussy.

She parted her legs wider and shook her head. "Holy shit! That's the biggest cock I've ever seen!"

A hand holding his appendage up at the threshold of Alex's pussy, he brought his other hand around her ass. "I'll be gentle, I promise," he said.

She still had one of her legs up on his shoulder, offering me the perfect vantage point. Watching his cock tease her was almost too much to bear from a distance. Its tip traced the groove between her swollen lips, not quite poking into her. My pussy ached; I wanted to feel him inside of me. My fingers, although swift and agile, paled in comparison to what I imagined he'd feel like in me.

Alex lowered her leg, partially obstructing my view. Then, the guttural roar she made as his ass moved forward a tad—probably just pushing the head of his humongous cock into her—made my heart skip a beat. Seemed the animal kingdom had also paused their soundtrack for a second.

Then she exhaled deeply and loudly twice like a Lamaze professional, then nodded at him.

"Okay. I'm ready. Give it to me. All of it."

And he pushed himself in. Her gorilla cries echoed against the nearby hills in the evening air. Her eyes rolled backward, then her entire head slammed back.

"Again!" she ordered.

He pulled out and slammed into her this time.

"Fuck, yeah!" she said. "Oh... Fuck me, Farmer John... Fuck me like there's no tomorrow."

And I watched him pound her, adding a third finger into my wet pussy. I groped my own breast with one hand, feeling even stronger ripples of desire building up inside of me.

"Wait, wait." Alex said in between two ramming sessions. "I want you to fuck me in the ass with your huge cock."

"Are you sure?" he asked.

"No, but who cares!"

He pulled out of her and rolled her onto her belly, letting her legs back down in the tub, and her ass pointed at him on the edge.

He parted her butt cheeks, then, with his other hand, brought up some of her pussy juice to her ass and let one finger in, then another, then another... A minute later, he was up to five fingers, slowly pushing in, loosening her anus, then he pulled his hand away and inserted himself into her.

Her roar made me wonder how much of it was pain vs. pleasure. Then, she turned to look his way, her eyes drunk on pleasure as each of his thrusts made her shrieks reach new heights.

When she turned her head back toward the front, our eyes met for an instant. She flinched every time he gave it to her, but her mouth stayed agape. She brought one hand under her stomach, then lifted her ass. Her eyes rolled back again as she let out a long squeal, her entire body shaking and spent. "Stop!" she begged.

He immediately pulled out of her. "Are you okay?" he asked Alex, his chest heaving up and down.

"Yeah. It's just so... big!"

"I know." He pulled his condom off, then, in a loud splash, sat himself back in the tub.

As though Alex had been reading my mind, she turned to look at me, then motioned for me to walk to them.

I left my towel behind and walked toward them, my own juices running down my right leg.

"But not all hope is lost," Alex said, now rolling unto her back, then sitting up. With a hand, she cupped her pussy, then lowered herself into the tub in front of him. She sent an inquisitive nod my way, her eyes round.

"Can I help?" I asked as I walked up the steps and joined them in the tub.

Farmer John's expression was priceless. He looked at Alex, then me, then Alex, and me again. "Really?" he finally asked.

"I'd love to feel your huge cock inside of me," I said.

"Then join us, please." He pointed to the empty seat next to Alex. I sat down, and he got up. His tool had deflated a bit from earlier, probably from Alex's request to stop, but that would likely be something easy to fix. I reached toward it, my eyes meeting his.

"Would you mind kissing her first?" he asked me.

I turned to Alex. She raised her shoulders then twisted her upper body to face me.

"You'd like that, wouldn't you?" I teased him. "Why not? Alex is beautiful."

I leaned in, put a hand behind her delicate neck, and briefly kissed her. Just a soft peck at first, but once I realized kissing my friend didn't feel weird, I started nibbling on her soft lips. I let my hand run through her red hair as my hunger for her grew. With a flick of my tongue, I parted her lips. Our breathing and excitement seemed to follow the same path toward the summit as our tongues mingled and our lips suckled. I reached for one of her gorgeous breasts under the water and gently cupped it, then my mouth departed from hers as I inched my way south, licking her ivory neck.

"Wait," she said. Her knees came up on the seat, then she pushed herself up on the edge where she sat and invited me to do the same.

I looked at Farmer John while I pulled myself out of the tub. His anaconda was now hard in the palm of his moving hand. I wanted to feel that part of him in me so badly. I reached a hand toward him, but Alex's fingers on my chin forced me to turn my head toward her.

Before I could say anything, her lips had swallowed mine again. Our breasts were now pressed against each other's. Then, out of the corner of my eye, I saw it. Inches from our faces was a cock so large it had to require a permit. Someone could lose an eye to it, if not lose themselves and be forever marked by it, comparing all future men to him.

I gently pushed Alex away from me as he moved forward between us.

We licked him. There was plenty for us to share as he was bigger than a large ear of corn—nothing any woman could fully wrap her mouth around. He tickled our tits while we did our best to suck and lick his humongous member. He tasted of chlorine, but that didn't do anything to deter my pussy's cravings.

Alex was a beautiful woman—and a fantastic

kisser—but what I wanted most in the world right now was Farmer John's cock in my swollen pussy.

"It's time. I'm ready." I parted my knees.

He reached to his discarded pants again then covered himself. His dick at the ready in front of me, his hand ran a recon mission in my pussy. I moaned the instant two of his fingertips entered my wet opening.

"More!" I ordered.

Farmer John pushed another finger in me and it slid in like it was nothing. I was so horny, it was no surprise to me.

"Come on. I want the real thing..." I begged.

He licked his lips as I parted my legs wider to make room for him. He moved his hips toward me until his tip knocked on my pleasure door.

I couldn't wait a second more, so I moved my weight to my hands behind my ass, and rammed myself onto his erect cock. It took me a second to realize that the scream I'd heard was mine. In a strange mix of pain and pleasure, I felt my insides somehow accommodating his large girth, parting ways and pushing outward. I then felt Alex's boobs against my back. She had relocated to sit behind me, her legs parted around my own legs. Her hands started to caress my upper body as I forcedly silenced myself.

My gaze locked onto Farmer John's, and I slowly moved back to rest my ass on the side of the tub, some of him still in me.

"More?" he asked.

I nodded and bit my lip, knowing full well I'd want to scream when he'd filled me again. Alex's caresses soothed me as he slowly started to increase his cadence, but not his depth. I was still controlling that by angling my hips, resting my weight on both of my hands, which I had to relocate behind Alex's legs since she was cradling me. Her right hand slowly made its way to my landing strip, then to my clit. As though she knew my body as well as hers, she started flicking my pleasure button. Her lips were nibbling on the back of my neck, her other hand pinching one of my nipples. Farmer John's huge dick pushing in and out of me like a giant smooth operator was just the cherry on top.

"I'm gonna come," I said.

"Hold on... A few more seconds," he said between thrusts, just as his breathing got louder and louder.

Then, in one final, painful push, he thrust into me fully. I'd lost control of my limbs while coming and hadn't been able to pull my hips back... But the pain had been worth it. I had never come so hard in my life. Maybe it was the high, maybe it was his girth and length, but I pulsated from everywhere. And, as he slowly pulled out of me, I realized how sensitive my entire pussy had become. From the orgasm... but possibly damaged by our encounter?

A few minutes later, too exhausted to do anything else, we returned to our tent.

8:30 A.M.

THE FOLLOWING MORNING, after dismantling our tent and stowing all our gear on our bikes, we kissed our farmer goodbye before saddling up again.

The trip back to town took us forever as we were both sore from riding the biggest cock we'd ever encountered.

# PART TWO

## MY XXX EXPERIENCE

# THE PLAN

WELL, Sophia wasn't generous with her leads this time. But here are my options:

**OPTION 1:** Go to Maastricht and track down the twins who own that coffee shop.

But for what purpose? I doubt she's keeping in touch since she couldn't even tell them apart when she left.

**Likelihood of success:** Nil.

**OPTION 2:** Find Farmer John.

Let's face it, I don't want to see that guy's face (or any other part of his body). I'd rather avoid proof that shows I'm not as far above the bell curve as I've always assumed I was.

**Likelihood of success:** Nil.

**OPTION 3:** Track down my stewardess based on her first name.

Since I got back from Paris with that important nugget, I haven't been able to sleep. While there's no way for me to know if she even works for my airline, it's worth a shot. I don't have access to the right people with other airlines. And maybe I'll get lucky. (And why wouldn't my streak continue?)

**Likelihood of success:** Low to average.

The last one is my only viable option.

And unfortunately, this means I won't go to Holland this time. As much as I like to pretend to be impulsive, I'm not. I'm a man of habits who thrives on standard operating procedures.

But maybe I'll hit the jackpot, find her, and end my quest. That would be worth so much more than sticking to my regular approach.

Bob keeps telling me I'm the luckiest guy alive. Let's see if he's right.

## WHAT HAPPENED

SO I GREASED the right wheels, bribed the right people, hired a hacker, and managed to get myself an official list of all flight attendants whose first names included Sophie, Sophia, Sofia, and even one Saufia. Whatever resembled her name, it got included on my list. I didn't want to risk missing her because of something Bob could have misheard. I got their full names, birthdates, and work history.

That was 49 of them.

Then, it was a matter of getting rid of those who didn't fit the bill physically or age-wise, although I couldn't be super precise with that last one. Facebook was a great help with this particular task, but only when my potential ladies included our common employer on their profile. I managed to get rid of a handful of blondes, a black woman, and a redhead.

A bit more unethical behavior from yours truly resulted in getting my remaining ladies' schedules, at least those who were senior enough to not fly reserve and hold their own line. My hacker worked his magic with the crew scheduler's account for that.

Then, several expensive bottles of whiskey were promised (and delivered) to a handful of my trustworthy colleagues who happened to fly the same routes as the remaining Sophias. Their sole task involved getting a selfie with that particular stewardess (or the entire crew if the solo shot was impossible). And if they couldn't deliver on that, then (and that was the least preferred option), a detailed description of what she looked like was provided.

Stalky a bit? Desperately so.

Illegal? Some parts definitely were.

But I was very careful and covered my tracks.

And it narrowed down my options to just three tall, thirty-something, curvy brunettes who required my personal attention and an in-person meeting.

But to save time and avoid extra work, I

compared their schedules and aircraft qualifications with the routes my stewardess had taken in her journal. Only one match remained; it had to be my mystery woman.

My illicit activities have paid off, and I've never had such a massive hard-on before.

I found myself a seat on her next flight the minute I had narrowed it down to her.

And guess what? I'm off to fucking Amsterdam/AMS.

*I can't believe it.*

I'm as lucky as Bob says I am. I can stick to my regular approach. I'm still pinching myself. After months obsessing about her, I'll meet my mysterious stewardess in the flesh in just a few hours.

Wish me luck.

6:15 P.M.

AS I TOOK my seat in the third row of the airplane, I spotted her helping a family stow their bags in the overhead compartments toward the back of the plane. Saying I had butterflies in my stomach didn't cut it; a full-fledged hurricane churned within me, and my heart threatened to pierce its way out of my chest cavity.

I forcefully inhaled and exhaled deeply as I took my seat. I placed my water bottle in the seat pocket in front of me and rested my shaky hands on my lap.

*This is it. Today's the day.*

But the right moment still had to come. More

and more people started crowding the aisle next to me, each slowly taking their assigned seat and storing their belongings away for the flight to come.

A minute after I had taken my seat, a scrawny man in a wrinkled business suit sat next to me.

"*Bonjour*," he said.

"Hi," I replied, recognizing one of the rare French words I knew.

After sliding his briefcase at his feet, he said something to me that I didn't get.

"Sorry, I only speak English," I said.

He frowned, then pressed his service button.

The nearest flight attendant, an older brunette whose white roots were showing, responded quickly, but she was also unable to understand and help him.

She lifted her index finger in the air. "Please wait, I'll get someone else to come and talk to you in French."

A few minutes later, *she* appeared, followed by a lovely flowery smell. Her hazel eyes landed on me, then my seat mate. She smiled at both of us with her luscious lips then said something in French.

*How lovely those lips were going to look when wrapped around my cock...*

The businessman requested whatever it was he

needed, and while he jabbered on, my eyes glanced at the name tag on her uniform: "Sophie". Her breasts, although hidden by the bulk of her uniform jacket, had to be solid Cs. Too bad X-ray vision wasn't a super-power of mine. I'd have liked to see her nipples to confirm she was indeed the one. But right when I considered speaking up, she walked away.

Probably good because I had no idea *what* I would have even said or asked.

I turned and stared at her ass as she headed toward the back of the plane. She was tall and curvy all right, pretty in a girl-next-door kind of way. Was her perfume jasmine-scented? I couldn't tell one flower scent from another, but she obviously spoke French.

Did I know her eyes were hazel? I couldn't recall that detail from her journal.

But she had to be my stewardess. She just had to.

*So... now what?*

*I can't mess this up.*

*What's my next move?*

*She's probably going to come back with whatever the Frenchman's requested, so how am I going to charm her off her feet?*

*What the hell can I say?*

No matter how many times I asked myself those questions, my mind always drew a blank larger than life. It was as though my smooth-talking skills had disappeared. My decades of successfully flirting with women forgotten and erased.

Where did my confidence go?

Had I jumped back to my teenage self?

In lieu of a clever pick-up line, the only thing that appeared in my mind was that hot autumn day in the neighborhood where I grew up.

I could see my own geeky self, unconfident, scrawny, long limbs, long hair. I'd been raking leaves on my neighbor's front lawn. She was so gorgeous. I can even recall what she wore on that specific day: a pair of ripped jean shorts with the white lining of the front pockets sticking out on her long, tanned thighs. Whenever she walked away from me, I would see the beautiful curves at the base of her round ass. Her old shirt had had its sleeves ripped out, half the buttons were undone, letting her ample bosom catch the last sun rays of that year's hot and humid Indian summer.

Although she always gave me a few dollars for taking care of various landscaping chores for her—like mowing the lawn, clearing eaves, or raking leaves—the real payment was seeing her body up close while she walked around or sat on her front porch. She sometimes wore a bikini or old overalls, but no matter what she had on, it always looked sexy on her.

But on that specific day in October, for raking her front lawn and bagging those dead leaves, she paid me by making a man out of me.

"When you're done, come in for some lemonade, will you?" she'd said to me before opening the squeaky screen door and walking into her house.

About five minutes later, three full bags of leaves carefully placed by the curb as she'd instructed me to, I walked up her front steps and let myself in.

"I'm done, Mrs. Thompson," I'd called out, unsure where she was. The kitchen table was bare. No freshly made pitcher of lemonade there.

"I'm in the living room."

After a few strides, I stepped into the framed opening that separated the kitchen from the living room, then I froze in place when I saw her. Mrs. Thompson was lying naked on her couch, one arm under her head. Everything I'd fantasized about for years was blatantly exposed for me to see: her large breasts, her tanned lines, her thick, untrimmed bush.

"Come here, Charles. Don't be afraid."

I remember hesitating, even though her voice had been soft and inviting.

After all, she was Mrs. Thompson, the hot divorcee my friends and I always talked about. Although I'd masturbated countless times with her in mind, seeing her naked in front of me was a different thing. Her body was even more beautiful than I had imagined. My boner had nowhere to hide, so it made its own tent out of the loose fabric of my gray sweatpants.

"I swear, I won't hurt you." Her red-hot manicured fingers were now making a come-here motion as irresistible as a mermaid's chant.

I still don't know how, but my legs somehow brought me next to her.

"Good, Charles. Now, I think you're wearing too many layers for such a hot day. Don't you think?"

I remember nodding, my mouth probably agape. I pulled my T-shirt over my head and tossed it at the edge of her glass-top coffee table.

She sat up and swung her body so her legs were

now parted, directly in front of me. Her pussy—my first one ever—had me hypnotized.

*So that's what it really looked like...*

Then, she'd broken the spell by pulling down my pants and underwear in one fell swoop.

"My, my. What have we got here, Charles? You're certainly all grown up now."

She'd been my babysitter over a decade ago, which confused yet aroused me even more. I tried to take another step closer to her, but tripped on myself. After a short fumble, I finally managed to kick off my shoes, then remove my sweatpants and underwear from around my ankles, leaving me completely naked save for a pair of white socks with blue stripes, which obviously became my lucky socks from that day onward.

"Don't be nervous," she said as she wrapped her warm hands around my waist.

My heart pounded in my chest as I reached toward her breasts. Although I'd lied and bragged about several other first and second bases to my buddies, that was my first official feel. I didn't know *how* I was supposed to touch her. My initial light graze soon turned into a full grope. I hadn't expected her breasts to feel so fleshy, so warm, so comfortable.

I kept squeezing them harder and harder, twisting them in my hand, until she covered my hands with hers and took them away from her beautiful body.

"Have you ever been with a woman, Charles?"

There was no point in lying. My lack of experience and knowledge would undoubtedly show sooner or later, so I shook my head.

"There's no shame in that. I'll show you, if you let me." Her eyes met mine and she wrapped one of her hands around my cock. "Do you want me to teach you, Charles?"

I don't recall verbally answering her, but I must have nodded or something. Come to think of it, my coming on her exposed breasts a second later may have been my only reply.

I remember apologizing profusely when she looked down at her chest, covered with streaks of my freshly squirted cum. With a finger, she traced a line through it, then brought that finger to her luscious pink lips. She'd opened her mouth slowly, then sucked my juices off from her finger while moaning.

"Let's try again, and this time, Charles, try to last a little longer... for my sake."

And I did my best.

That time, and the time after that. And the time after that.

For the rest of that afternoon, she did things to me that I'd only seen blurred through the channels we didn't get at home. And each time I came, I'd learned new things and lasted a little longer.

That's how October 15, 1992 saw the death of Charles the geek and the birth of Charlie the stud.

The following day at school, I not only got to brag to the rest of the chess club that I had lost my virginity, but I got to say that I'd lost it to Mrs. Thompson, the sexy, hot neighborhood divorcee. She was a MILF well before that term even got coined.

But right now, more than two decades later, Mrs. Thompson was nowhere to be seen.

It was just me, sitting on a crowded plane, with stupid Charles somehow having taken the controls again. I was unable to think of anything clever to say to Sophie. I drew a fucking blank. No charming remarks came to my lips. Nothing at all.

How could this be? After months spent looking for her, tracking her down, having out-of-this world sexual encounters... Had my impossible quest somehow moved my mystery stewardess up onto a pedestal?

*Get your shit together, Charlie.*

*She's just a woman, not a goddess. A regular human being, like you, but with nice tits, a starving pussy... and sexual cravings that expand well beyond your own horizons.*

I SPENT the rest of the flight trying to exorcise geeky Charles and come up with a plan. But looking at the napkin onto which I'd scribbled my best lines, none of them seemed interesting, clever, or charismatic enough.

*And I don't fucking know what her plans are.*

*I'll have to wing it, hoping that good ole Charlie will reappear, step up, and bring my macho confidence back up to snuff.*

At least luck was still on my side as I managed not to lose track of her once we disembarked and cleared customs. I was even within earshot when she mentioned to one of her colleagues that she was staying at the CitizenM airport hotel.

That was all I needed for my next step. I headed there directly since I could hardly hang around any longer in close proximity to her and her colleagues without them noticing my unwelcome presence.

And luck came back to me once more. She arrived at the check-in desk just after I finished checking myself in.

"Sophie, right?" I said with a large smile, then offered my hand. "I'm Charlie."

She shook it in silence, her head tilted to the side, a slight frown on her face.

"I'm a pilot. I think we've flown together before," I said in a tone that came out more like a question than a fact.

"I don't think so," she finally said.

"Are you sure? You seem really familiar."

"Is this why you were looking at me during the flight?"

So much for what I thought had been discreet looks. "Sorry, I was just trying to place you."

Her phone buzzed, and she flipped it to look at the screen.

Afraid that my chance was going to squeeze through my fingers right there and then, I launched my best effort. "Want to grab a coffee or something?" I asked, mentally hating my lame approach while my heart started pounding in expectation.

"Hmm," she said, her eyes glued on her screen. She typed something, then finally looked up at me again.

"Well... I was supposed to be picked up by a friend, but I just got a text saying there's been a delay. I guess I have a few hours to kill now, so why not? I'll let you buy me coffee, and we can try and figure out if you actually know me from somewhere."

"Sounds fair," I said, hopeful. "I'll let you check in, and then we can meet down here in about ten minutes?"

"Better make it twenty. I want to freshen up and get out of my uniform."

AFTER TAKING my carry-on up to one of the most modern-looking, minimalist room I've seen in a long time, I went in for a quick cold shower, put on a pair of jeans and a polo shirt, and then had a good chat with myself in front of the mirror. I won't repeat my ruthless words here—I doubt I could remember everything I yelled at my reflection—but let's just say that, hands down, I would have won the World's Harshest Drill Sergeant prize.

Now completely re-invigorated and psyched, I was confident that good ole Charlie was ready to kick that wuss of a ball-less, teenage Charles out of me and play hard core. But I still had no room for errors, or else it would mean the end of it. I certainly didn't want my quest to finish in such a disappointing way.

I checked my watch: another five minutes to go. With nothing else for me to do in my room (unless I wanted to turn on the television and risk losing track of time), I headed down to the main floor.

It wasn't just my room that didn't look like the typical hotel. The entire lobby and lounge area had benefited from the same out-of-the-box thinking. Food and drinks were available 24/7 and the assortment of furniture and decorations around me felt like I was in some bizarro, wealthy man's living room filled with eclectic artwork, several bookcases serving as partitions, and interesting, contemporary artwork.

I was about to take a seat in a low, IKEA-like chair when Sophie appeared, small purse in hand and dressed in white capri pants with a light blue blouse. She'd tied her long brown hair in a ponytail. I resisted the urge to check my watch, but I believe she was right on time. *Good girl.*

I walked over to meet her halfway. I noticed she'd put on more makeup than she'd worn earlier on the plane. Her hazel eyes had somehow been highlighted more, and the curvature of her lips was even more tempting in the darker, almost burgundy shade she'd put on. So glossy and inviting...

"What are you in the mood for?" I asked.

"Coffee and... some sort of breakfast sandwich would be good."

"Let's see what they have." I pointed to the restaurant and followed her, admiring her curves from behind for just a second before returning my attention to the selection of food offered to us.

She found what she was looking for: coffee with a ham-and-cheese croissant. After the airplane breakfast—not that it had been particularly spectacular—I wasn't hungry, so I only grabbed a black coffee. I added it all to my room, then we made our way to the sitting area where we picked a small two-person table away from the other people currently enjoying their late-morning breakfasts.

After eating, Sophie pulled out her phone, a small moleskin notebook, and a pen from her purse. She checked her phone, then moved to the notebook and quickly wrote down something in it. She closed it before I could even glance at her handwriting (or see what she'd noted).

*It doesn't look like the diary I have, but maybe she writes down notes in this small book and later transfers them to her diary?*

"I don't want to be nosy," I said, "but can I ask what you just wrote down?"

She looked at me with a puzzled look. "Oh! Just a thought I didn't want to forget."

"Like a note-to-self?" I joked.

"Guess so. It's for something I'm writing."

*God, it's definitely her.*

She put her notebook and pen back in her purse. "So..." she said, her eyes wide open, "You've got my full attention now."

"I'm still trying to place you. How long have you flown with our airline?"

"Coming up on twelve years."

"Then we must have crossed paths at some point, no?"

Her phone beeped and she lifted it to read something on her screen.

"Married? Boyfriend?" The minute the words left my lips I realized my questions were too personal, too fast. "I mean, the messages you're getting. Are they from your husband or boyfriend?" I nodded toward her phone.

"No! No such man in my life, but you're almost right. The messages are from someone I've been communicating with for a while. We'll be meeting for the first time in person today. At least, we're supposed to."

"Oh. You met on a dating site?"

"Sort of..." she said.

I didn't know where to go with this line of questioning. Had I found her just in time? Just before she was about to meet another man that could be right for her? Her phone beeped again before I could ask a follow-up question.

"Damn..." she said.

"Another delay?"

"Yes." She frowned and shook her head, obviously annoyed.

"I can keep you company for a little longer if you'd like."

She looked up from her screen for a second. "Really?" she asked. "Don't you have people to meet, places to go?"

"I'm meeting you right now," I said with my largest panty-dropping smile.

"Hmmm..." Her face showed no sign of delight; her eyebrows and smile were as flat as the country we were in. *What? She's immune to my charisma?* "Is this supposed to be a 'living in the moment' kind of reply?" she finally asked.

"You could say that."

*How can my mysterious stewardess be this ball-busting*

*in real life? Did I create a fantasy not a single woman could ever live up to? Not even* her?

Her face became that of a dramatic interviewer. "Seriously, why did you come to Amsterdam?"

"I'm following a trail."

"Hmmm. Detective work? Didn't you say you're a pilot?"

For a second, I saw a flash of curiosity in her eyes. "Something personal I'm looking into."

"And why aren't you looking into that thing or meeting someone if you flew all the way here?"

*Careful, Charlie.* "I need to figure out my next move."

"Ahh, so you're also stuck in limbo here?"

"You could say that." *Fuck, this isn't going as planned.* I looked at the bottom of my empty coffee cup. "So, what do you think? Considering our mutual limbo status, how does having another drink with me sound?"

Her shoulders went up. "Guess it'd be fine. It would probably prevent my mind from spinning into a stressful spiral of *what-ifs.*"

"Great. But I got to be honest, I don't think I can have another cup of coffee without starting to shake, so how about a cold beer?"

She raised her shoulders. "Why not?"

"Do you have time to make it into town?"

She typed a reply on her phone and waited a few seconds before answering me. "Looks like it. Terry mentioned an early flight tonight."

*Terry, so that's the name of my competitor...*

"It's settled then. Let's go and be tourists in Amsterdam."

"HAVE YOU EVER CYCLED THROUGH HERE?" I asked her as a few cyclists passed by us at a leisurely pace.

"Around Amsterdam? Sure. Best way to tour the city."

"No, I mean the rest of the country?"

"I've seen parts of it. Not all of it for sure."

"Did you come across... huge surprises?"

"Huge surprises?" she scrunched her face at me. "Depends on what you mean—"

Her phone beeped again and she stopped walking to read the message that had appeared on her screen.

I stopped as well, unsure what to do.

A second later she started typing away, her head shaking faster and faster. Then another beep sounded, likely signaling the arrival of another message. She shook her head again, pressed a button, and then started talking into her phone: "Just text me when you get here then. I've left the airport and I'm walking around Amsterdam."

*Voice message to the mysterious Terry?*

I stood still and inhaled deeply, using the opportunity to refocus.

*Cat's got your tongue, Charlie? Here's your chance. She's fucking stuck with you. Can't you think of something flirty to say? Can't you come up with one single fucking line that will work on her? Wake the fuck up!*

"Sorry," she said after putting her phone in her purse. "What were we talking about?"

"Can't remember. Are you flying back out tomorrow?" I asked.

"Yeah, tomorrow evening. I was supposed to explore Amsterdam with Terry today and tomorrow. At least that was the plan..."

We resumed walking, this time in silence. I had no idea what was going through her mind, but I knew I was moving on quicksand; my opportunity with Sophie was dissipating fast.

"So, you've got children?" I asked once we'd taken a seat at a table on a busy patio.

She shook her head. "Nah, I don't have the patience nor the desire to proliferate."

"But you must like practicing the art, no?" I suggested with what I intended to be lascivious eyes.

She blushed, kept quiet, and returned her attention to the menu.

*There's my blushing stewardess!* The speed at which her cheeks had reddened surprised me... And ignited my carnal desires faster than a gallon of gasoline would have warmed up a lit fire.

"I'll get a glass of Merlot," she finally said. "What about you? See something you like?"

I met her eyes. "Definitely."

Her cheeks flushed to an even darker shade of red. "On the menu?"

"Sure, I'll have a Heineken."

After putting in our orders, a couple of minutes lapsed into an awkward silence.

*What is it about her that prevents me from being myself?*

And just then, a particularly strong breeze brought along a skunky scent. *Time to bet it all on black.*

"How about trying a coffee shop after our drinks?"

"You're kidding, right? We can't go in one of those places," she said.

"There's nothing wrong with having a look." I tried to gauge her expression. Was she really offended, or was she just a good actress? I *knew* she smoked weed on a semi-regular basis. "Are you worried someone could see us and report us to the Aviation Board?"

"Duh... Yeah!"

I shrugged. "We could claim we thought it was a regular coffee shop?"

"Do it if you want, but I'm not going to go anywhere near it. I like my job too much to risk it."

I waved my hand in the air. "No worries, forget I even mentioned it." And just then, I saw the waitress appear with a tray. "Let's just enjoy our drinks."

*Lifesaving timing, really.* The gap between my stewardess and me widened with each passing second she stared at me with her scrunched-up face.

I lifted up my drink and offered a toast: "To the lucky ones like us who get to work in the sky."

She kept frowning at me, but nonetheless clinked her glass against my bottle. Not a word escaped her lips.

As I brought my cold beer to my lips a second

later, I identified the source of the sinking feeling in my stomach.

*She doesn't know who I am!*

She sipped her wine in silence, her attention turned toward nearby patrons who were having a lively discussion about something or other.

*Contrary to my hopes, she didn't choose me that fateful day when her journal appeared in my bag. My becoming the new (and proud) owner of her diary was just luck. Random fucking luck.*

I sipped my beer, glancing at her, then taking in my surroundings while my brain tried to continue its analysis. *Because she doesn't know who I am, it makes sense for her to worry about me reporting her being in a coffee shop and getting her in trouble.* After all, it had been my initial intention... until I got addicted to her and her sexual experiments.

But my inner-jabber—combined with the lack of sleep during the previous night's red-eye flight—threatened to give me a headache, so I put an end to it all.

"Sophie," I said loudly, trying to gain her attention again from whatever she was looking at.

She turned to look at me, her expression flat, save for her raised eyebrows.

"Tell me about your worst passenger ever."

A faint smile finally appeared on her face.

*Good. Not all hope is lost.*

"So many to choose from. Let me think..."

She brought her glass up and took a sip. For a second, the wine moistened her luscious lips, making them look even more enticing. But then she smacked them, and they were dry again. She put her glass down and smiled at me.

"I got one. On a flight to Madrid, about three years ago, there was this one, very odd man. I mean, the guy looked like he was a hundred years old, but he was dressed like a teenager. Mind you, a teenager from a few decades earlier. He had on a black AC/DC T-shirt, ripped bleached jeans, that kind of clothing, you know?" She paused and took another sip.

"You got me intrigued. Go on," I said.

"So, it was after takeoff, but before we'd reached our cruising altitude. So the guy starts yelling—"

Her phone beeped. Again.

She picked it up from the table and, after a few seconds spent reading her screen, she recorded another voice message: "This is getting absurd. Why don't we meet at the Unicorn like we'd discussed? Ten o'clock?"

*Duly noted.*

She returned her phone to the table. "Sorry about that."

"No problem. So what did the guy start yelling about?"

Her phone beeped again, which drew a deep line between her brows. "I'm sorry. I gotta call Terry. This is getting ridiculous."

So I watched her get up and walk away from me, phone in hand.

She'd left her purse on the table though. The very purse that contained the small notebook she'd written in earlier today... Within seconds, if I acted quickly, I would be able to see her handwriting. I'd be able to read what she's been taking notes about...

But as I slowly moved my hand toward it on the table, I decided against it. I closed my hand into a fist and brought it back closer to my body.

*That's not right. If I even want to stand a chance at getting to know her better, I have to respect her privacy.*

Instead, I turned my attention to her. She stood quite a few steps away from me now, out of earshot, but I could see the phone against her ear and her arm flailing in the air.

*Poor Terry.* That guy may be even worse off than me! That Sophie certainly doesn't like being stood up.

I'd finished my beer by the time she came back.

Her face flushed, she emptied the remainder of her glass and said, "Sorry. I gotta go."

She grabbed her purse, and started digging around, probably for cash.

"No problem. Don't worry about the drink. It's on me."

She let out a sigh and stopped digging through her purse. "Thanks." She took a step away, then turned to me and said, "Enjoy your stay in Amsterdam."

"Same for you."

And that had been it. Probably my worst attempt at flirting with a woman on record. Disgruntled, I left more than enough money to cover my bill on the table, then headed back to my hotel room.

I had to regroup and get my game plan on if I wanted to impress her at the Unicorn tonight.

9:50 P.M.

AFTER A LONG AFTERNOON NAP, I Googled the location of the Unicorn, then showed up there, dressed for success. Well, dressed in my best jeans and a sharp black shirt.

But the moment I stepped into the bar, some powerful vibe threw me off. Loud dance music made my eardrums shake, and neon light beams bounced off of various mirrored surfaces, almost blinding me in the process. The crowd was made up of young, overly-perfumed, well-manicured men and women. But mostly men.

I couldn't see Sophie just yet, but I spotted the bar and headed toward it as it seemed like the best observation point for now.

As I walked in that direction, the screen that hung above the young barman got my attention. It currently displayed an exercise video featuring five men in tiny, tight, fluorescent-colored spandex outfits. Not a single woman in that shot. Whether it was an original from the 80s or a remake in that style, the muscular men wore very little fabric. I had to look away.

Then, someone tapped me on the shoulder. I turned around and a tall, slender blond man was staring at me.

"Hi! Want to dance?" he asked as he moved his hips and arms—or at least, that's what I heard over the loud music.

"No, thanks." As I shook my head at him, it finally dawned on me.

*Why is Sophie meeting that Terry guy in a gay bar? Or did I mishear the bar's name?*

I turned away from the blond man—he was still looking at me, a wide smile on his lips. I turned to face the bar and dug my phone out of my pocket. A few minutes spent trying to find similar-sounding bar names proved fruitless. I looked at my watch: almost ten o'clock.

While I was definitely not hanging out in my favorite place in the world, I could stand the environment a few minutes longer. I couldn't leave without giving all I had trying to get into Sophie's pants. After all of these months...

I waved at the bartender and ordered myself a beer, then sat myself at a small table that had just become empty.

I was halfway through my drink when Sophie finally appeared, a tall, spiky-haired blonde in tow.

*Did Terry cancel on her? When did she meet that woman?*

Beer in hand, I walked up to them just as Sophie's woman friend left the table in direction of the bar.

*Shit, wait. Terry can also be a girl's name...*

"I need to talk to you," I said a couple of inches from her ears. I put my drink down in front of her.

"You? What are you doing here?" Her voice pitched high enough for me to hear it over the thump of the dance music.

I leaned in close to her right ear. "I can't stop thinking about you. Everything you wrote in your diary—"

"My diary?" She turned to face me, displaying a frown seemingly made of anger and confusion "How? When?"

I backed off, my hands in the air. "Hey, hey!

Relax!" I closed the gap again so she could hear me over the loud music. "You're the one who left it in my briefcase, remember?"

She winced at me, then shook her head. "What are you talking about?"

"Canada, Mexico, Costa Rica, Los Angeles, Ireland, Thailand, France, and now here. Your entries—"

"What's wrong with you? I've never given you my diary. And I've never ever been to Thailand. You've obviously got me confused with someone else... Creep!"

"But you speak French. Your name's Sophia and you match her description to a—"

"My name's Sophie, not Sophia. I've got no idea who you're looking for, but it's obviously not me. You're a stalker. That's what you are."

The blonde woman came back to the table, two beers in hand, condensation already beading down the sides of the bottles. I didn't like that woman a bit. Something seemed off about her, and it wasn't the weird piercings that decorated her face. She eyed me down with a look of disdain, but the feeling was mutual.

"I'm Terry. Who are you?" she asked.

"Nobody," Sophie replied before turning to me. "Now get away from me or I'm calling the cops."

I waved my empty hands in front of me. "No need. I'm gonna finish my drink and leave you alone."

I grabbed the nearest bottle and walked back to my own table. I'd already taken a few steps too many to back track when I realized I'd taken the wrong bottle. The one I held was full and cold.

*Fuck them. Let it be my consolation prize.*

*But how the fuck did I get so misled? Did she lie to me?*

I returned to my previous table and sat while staring at her and that Terry woman from a distance. With each sip, I reviewed my steps, my process, my assumptions...

That was it: I'd *assumed* too many things. I'd seen what I'd wanted to see. But now, watching them together, I got annoyed. Annoyed at my own stupidity. The more I drank, the more ashamed I got. Then again, no wonder I wasn't able to flirt with her. She's a fucking lesbian.

*Well fuck it, fuck her.*

I got up and nearly toppled over, so I sat right back down.

*Whoa. What the fuck?*

I blinked hard, then reopened my eyes. The neon beams that flashed around me now had blurred edges, the floor had taken on an angle, or so it seemed... Then a wave of nausea forced me up on my feet again, so I ran to the men's room, tripping and colliding against a few people on the way, but I nonetheless reached the back of the bar. I pushed the door open and barely had time to get in the nearest stall—thankfully vacant—and I emptied my gut in a loud reverberation. The cold porcelain under my hands and the overpowering scent of bleach mixed with urinal cakes just added to my confusion.

"Are you okay?" a man's voice asked behind me.

I puked once more, then turned around. Once my blurred vision settled, I realized he was that tall blond man who'd asked me to dance earlier.

I couldn't articulate my thoughts. Words danced in my head, but my tongue was tangled and unable to move, so I just shook my head.

"Come with me, I'll help you," he said with an open palm. "I'm Frank."

I tried to grab his hand, but my vision had gotten worse. He grabbed me by the waist and lifted me up from the floor. "Do your best to stand up. I'll walk you out." He then wrapped an arm around me and guided me out of the bathroom.

*Frank...*

I tried to concentrate so I could remember his name while he guided me out of the bar.

The last thing I remember is seeing a cab pull over.

I WOKE up in a very bright room, with sun shining in through the sheer curtains. My head and my entire face hurt. My mouth tasted of vomit.

After blinking a few times, my vision got clearer, but none of the furniture around me looked familiar. I was in a beautiful, modern-looking room alright, but it wasn't the room I'd checked in the day before in the hotel.

A clank of dishes echoed nearby.

*Where the fuck am I?*

I looked down at the mangled sheets. Below my naked chest, my morning erection stood proud and bare, as always. Without a clue as to where I was, how I'd gotten here, and who I'd spent the night with, I looked around the room once more for any hint. My own clothing had been piled and carefully folded on top of a large leather chair in the corner. Even my boxer briefs.

*Well, that's a first.*

I swung my legs out and tried to get up, but I had to sit again until the room stopped spinning. My face and jaw were super sore. On my second attempt, I managed to slowly get up and walk around the room, but no lacy bra or panties were in sight. In fact, nothing seemed out of place in this tidy bedroom, save for me and my neat little pile of clothing on the chair.

I proceeded to get dressed, but I'd only donned my underwear when I heard a knock.

"Are you awake?" asked a man's voice from behind the door.

I froze for a second, then looked at the room again. Although decorated with taste, it showed absolutely no feminine touches: no decorative throw pillows, no flowers of any kind, no shades of pink. This was a man's bedroom.

Then the name *Frank* came back to mind.

*Who the fuck is Frank?*

I put on my jeans and shirt before opening the door to see who that man was, but whoever had knocked no longer stood there. But I heard more clinking noises so I followed the smell of fresh coffee, which directed me toward the kitchen.

"Ha! You are awake. Good morning," said the tall blond man standing in front of the stovetop. Taller than me, but skinnier. His tousled hair made me believe he too had recently woken up.

*Better not have shared the same bed...*

He seemed friendly enough, although I still didn't understand or recall how I knew him or how I got here.

"What the fuck is going on? Who are you and where am I?"

"Social etiquette is obviously not your strong suit, but I can't blame you, I guess. I'm Frank, an American ex-pat," he said, letting go of the pan he was holding and extending his hand toward me.

I shook it, probably out of habit. "Charlie," I said.

"Nice to meet you officially, Charlie."

"So... Frank... Why am I here? What did you do to me?"

He shook his head, then flipped the pancake he was cooking. "Me? I was just a good Samaritan. Someone spiked your drink last night."

*Spiked my drink?*

*That would explain the stumbling and whatever I could barely recall.*

Now I remembered him asking me to dance. "And it wasn't you?"

"Pleeeaase. I understand the meaning of no."

My instinct told me he wasn't lying, but that alone didn't answer any of my many unresolved questions. "So who did?" I asked.

"Coffee?" he offered.

I shook my head; my stomach wasn't ready for coffee yet. "You have water?"

"Sure," he said before opening his fridge. "Flat or sparkling?"

"Flat's fine."

He handed me a bottle, still sealed. "I think it was that spiky-haired chick with the piercings. Although I don't believe you were the intended target. Weird friends you have."

I downed half the bottle he'd handed me and let its refreshing, cold liquid parch my thirst while the information sank in.

"But how would you know this?"

"You caught my eye last night, so I was curious about you. Watched you for a bit. I don't know the story behind that little love triangle you're involved with, but that girl with the piercings seemed to have something against you. Then—"

"Did you see her spike my beer?"

"No. I didn't. But you looked sober when I approached you earlier. A guy of your size getting that disoriented after a beer or two could only be explained by a handful of reasons. And I've unfortunately seen it before, so I knew in an instant."

"And you didn't call the police?"

"You were in no shape to stay and wait for the police to show up. Even less able to explain what had happened to you. I had no idea where you lived or if you were a tourist staying in a hotel. I wasn't going to start searching you for a hotel card key or driver's license. I figured the best option was to take you somewhere safe while you could still walk. Barely."

"Well... I guess I should thank you, then? But why the fuck did you get me naked?"

"No, that was all you. I swear I didn't touch you. You got naked all on your own. Man, I get your lack of trust here, you've obviously got something against homosexuals, but go ahead. Look in your wallet. I didn't steal anything from you."

And I did. I checked my pockets, dug my wallet

out and opened it. My ID, credit cards, money... Everything was accounted for. I checked my wrist and noticed my watch was missing.

"My watch?"

"You took it off last night. Sorry, I forgot to place it with your clothes. It must still be in the living room. We can have a look later. You want breakfast?"

"Why is my face hurting so damn much?"

"You don't remember that? Go have a look at yourself in the mirror," he said, pointing toward a door down the hallway.

I walked over to the bathroom and shrieked when I saw my reflection. Shades of purple and blue covered my right eye and upper cheek. "What the heck? Did you do that to me?" I yelled out toward the kitchen.

"To your pretty face? Never in a million years. Your big mouth got you in trouble before we got in the cab."

I walked back to the kitchen to hear the rest of his story. "What do you mean?"

"Given that you were rapidly losing it, I skipped the taxi line. One guy made a comment you didn't like, then you called him a faggot, among several other homophobic insults. You probably got what

119

you deserved there... Especially if you consider you were leaving a gay bar. That black eye's on you. You actually had me rethink saving your ass, and I didn't want to go to the police because I didn't know if the guys you swung at were going to press charges..."

The reality of what had happened slapped me in the face just as he slid a pancake on one of the empty plates on the table. "Eat something. It'll help."

I took a seat. "Fuck... Sorry, man. And thank you for saving my ass." I poured some syrup onto the pancake then cut away my first bite.

I FIGURED I had to do one thing right now. I had about six hours to kill before my return flight, and I might as well use my time wisely so I could get back on the figurative horse.

So I headed down De Walden in broad daylight.

*Gotta love a place where à-la-carte sex is openly and easily available, almost 24 hours a day.*

After meandering for a few blocks, I spotted the right girl for me. A young brunette with curvy hips and a coy smile stood in a red window in a tiny emerald-green bikini. Her big round eyes matched her outfit. A wink was all it took to convince me to head over to her.

She opened the door, keeping her body protected and hidden by it, and she smiled at me.

"Hello. You want to come in?" she asked with an accent I couldn't place.

"Of course. You look lovely, but what will you do to me and how much will it cost?"

She eyed me up and down. "For you? Fifteen minutes: a blow job and a fuck for sixty euros."

*Fair price to bring my ego back up.*

I nodded, and she stepped aside to clear the door.

I walked in and inhaled her powdery perfume. She leaned in to close the door and draw the curtain. She led me up a short flight of stairs, then opened a door and invited me to step in.

The small bedroom smelled of sex and incense and was flooded with a warm, red tone that came from a couple of tall floor lamps in the corner. A washroom had been built-in without a need for partition: a small sink, toilet, and bidet occupied a corner of the room. A queen-sized bed lined with burgundy sheets reigned in front of me on a raised platform. The main wall behind the bed and the ceiling above us were covered with mirror tiles. My own discolored reflection met my eyes and I looked away.

"Pay first," she said after closing the bedroom door.

I dug out my wallet and retrieved three twenty-euro bills, which she grabbed from my hand before sending me a large smile. "Thank you."

Well aware that the clock had already started ticking, I took off my shirt and pants in record time, leaving them jumbled on the floor.

My green-eyed woman, on the other hand, wasn't in such hurry.

As I made my way to the bed where she now sat, her long legs partly folded in front of her, she pulled at the string behind her neck, slowly undoing the knot of her top. She then pulled down on one side of the strings, exposing one of her gorgeous breasts.

Standing at the foot of the bed, I reached toward her and pulled down on the other side. I let her fleshy goodness fill my hands and reinvigorate my bruised ego. After all, it was no secret—at least to me—that women and their curves were the cure to the majority of men's problems.

"What's your name?" I asked her.

"Call me Luisa."

I had the feeling that it wasn't her real name, but I didn't care. I let go of her breasts and pulled on the strings that held her bottom tied. A second later, I pulled it down and exposed her trimmed brown bush. She scooted up and sat on the edge of the bed, parting her knees to wrap her legs around mine. I liked her 'do: she'd left a small triangular welcome mat above her fully shaven pussy.

Her warm mouth went directly for my cock, engulfing my erect girth and making me forget where I was.

I let out a grunt and tilted my head back, meeting the reflection of our naked bodies on the ceiling. Her head bobbed in front of me at an irregular pace. When she pulled back to where I was barely in her mouth, I could see her breasts between us, then she blew cool air on my cock before swallowing it again. I wrapped my hands around the back of her head, her silky hair slipping between my fingers as I moved her head up and down to my preferred cadence.

Cold fingers got a hold of my balls, surprising me a little, but what she did with them more than made up for it.

My own grunts echoed in the room, her slurping sounds accompanying them as I approached my point of no-return.

"I want to come on your tits," I ordered as I let go of her head.

And she moved back on the bed to become a beautiful target, her arms holding her back up at the perfect angle for me to aim at. I wrapped my hand around my shaft and made myself come, splattering her gorgeous tits with all of my might. Pleased with my tension having finally been released, I looked up at her and that's when I noticed the void behind her gaze, an indescribable look that experienced sex workers often shared.

It was business after all.

She didn't know me from Adam.

I didn't pay her enough to care and pretend to like me.

And I was fine with that.

She got up on her knees and massaged her own breasts, letting my juices spread on her pale skin.

"You want to fuck me now?"

"Give me a minute, and I'll be ready," I said. "Turn around and get on all fours."

"Anal is more," she said to me, not budging.

"Don't worry, just regular doggy style."

She nodded. "But let me cover you up."

"Let me see your ass first."

She obeyed and got on all fours in front of me.

Seeing her ripe peach winking at me like that had me ready to go again. I was putting my hands on her hips, prepared to act, but she lowered herself to the bed. She stretched out and reached to grab a condom.

She ripped it open with her teeth, then pulled it out of the wrapper, holding it in her mouth. She made her way back to me, on her knees, and then pushed the condom onto the tip of my erect cock with her mouth. Then, she unraveled it with her lips and tongue. Practiced trick or not, I was impressed.

Cock covered and more than ready to enjoy the rest of my paid interlude, I motioned for Luisa to turn around. On all fours in front of me, her ass was sublime; her pussy, inviting; her scent, intoxicating. I parted then massaged her butt cheeks, then lowered my thumbs to her warm, pink pussy. She was wet and ready.

"We don't have all day. Fuck me," she ordered.

And I obeyed, first just dipping into her, pleasantly surprised at her tightness, then I rammed the rest of my length into her warmth. I got a hold of her hips, then parted my legs a bit to lower myself and began pushing out all of my frustration, as if each thrust somehow erased my most recent mistakes. Luisa's hair fell forward, hiding her face in the reflection in the mirror in front of us and, for an instant, I saw Mrs. Thompson naked in front of me.

For a moment, I allowed myself to relive what that had been like. She'd taught me to do it doggy style. I'd gotten bad carpet burns on my knees from doing her on all fours in her living room.

Bit by bit, as I watched the beautiful woman in front of me arch her back, hearing her breasts flap against her own skin, catching a glimpse of them bouncing in the mirror in front of us, Luisa and my memories of Mrs. Thompson morphed together and finally exorcised Charles out.

And when I came in my final thrust, it was Charlie's doing. I was back. My ego healed, my hopes to find the right Sophia somehow heightened.

"FINALLY GOT what was coming to you?" a woman's voice asked a few feet from me.

I turned slightly and recognized Sophie.

"How's Terry?" I tried to smile, but my bruised cheek made me wince instead.

"Looks painful." Her hand went up as if to touch my face, but she dropped it by her side instead. "Unsure if you deserved that. I should thank you for walking away with my beer that night. Because of you, I avoided whatever Terry was going to do to me. Steal my passport, money, kidney... who knows?"

"So it really was her who'd spiked it?"

She nodded. "And she even had the balls to try

it again. But by the time she ordered me a new beer and got back to my table, I saw you stumbling away. I put two and two together and didn't touch it. I threatened to call the cops and she ran out. I suspect I'll never hear back from her. Do you want her contact info so you can report her to the cops?"

"No, but thanks for offering. A... friend helped me out. Don't know how my night would have ended if he hadn't stepped in. And sorry for how I treated you. I really thought you were someone else."

"Another woman deserves to be stalked like that?"

I let out a long sigh. "It's not like that. It's not what you think."

"Well, good luck with that," Sophie said before smiling at me and joining the rest of her crew who were already boarding the plane.

## NEXT STEPS

WELL, I haven't found her after all, and I definitely got my ass kicked in more ways than one.

Thank goodness there are still good people like Frank out there. No hidden agenda, no rape, no theft, nothing. Just a good person with a good heart. I respected him for that. I'm not sure I would have done the same if our roles had been reversed.

I guess I have some growing up to do. And while that black eye heals, I'll have a visual reminder of the asshole I can sometimes be.

So while I'm not back to square one, I'm nowhere closer to meeting her. But I know she doesn't work for my airline and that's something.

I could start hitting on all brunettes that wear

uniforms from other airlines. My dick could go limp trying to find her...

Or I could use her unbelievable journal entries from Japan to try and narrow it down some more. The weird shit she's done—which was recorded on video—is just mind-blowing.

Those crazy Japanese game shows are just... incredible.

TO BE CONTINUED...

...IN PART 9 of *The Stewardess's Diary*, available at most major book retailers.

The complete episodic novel is also available in one (thick) paperback with exclusive author's notes about the series and what inspired each episode.

## ABOUT THE AUTHOR

S.M. Pratt is a single woman traveling the world on her own, living in the moment, looking for more than love, and always trying out new things. Fun adventures and unique cultural experiences are always at the top of her agenda, no matter the country she happens to be visiting.

She would love to quit her day job and write full-time. You can help her write the next story faster by purchasing her books and/or giving her five-star reviews. Without your support, she's invisible and unable to make a living doing what she loves, which is creating what you love to read.

If you haven't done so already, please join her private reader group for previews, exclusive offers, and more. It's free: https://smpratt.com

*For more information:*
smpratt.com
info@smpratt.com

www.ingramcontent.com/pod-product-compliance
Lightning Source LLC
Chambersburg PA
CBHW020916180626
46816CB00007BA/2420